CU00863513

For my nephew Michael – D.D.

For my son Valentín – C.B.

Published in the United States by Stone Hollow Press, a NY-based entertainment and publishing company.

Visit: www.stonehollowpress.com

First Edition: May 2021

ISBN 978-1-7341771-0-7 (hardcover)
ISBN 978-1-7341771-1-4 (paperback)

The Little Brown Spider: Which Way to Go? / Written by Dennis DeRobertis ; illustrated by Cristian Bernardini.

Summary: The Little Brown Spider helps a young boy overcome his fear of finding his classroom on the first day of school.

About our Mascot

"Often talked about, but rarely seen, this majestic, yet elusive creature is said to inhabit the hills and trails of New York's beautiful Hudson Valley region.

"One could easily mistake it for a common crow if not for its slightly larger size and odd coloring. It is dressed in vibrant orange feathers, with lighter ones adorning its crest.

"When spotted, it is often atop an old growth stump of a once mighty red maple. Most sightings occur in the fall, especially around Halloween.

"It is known as The Pumpkrin or Pumpkin Crow."

The Little Brown Spider in

Which Way to Go?

Written by

Dennis DeRobertis

Illustrated by

Cristian Bernardini

Stone
Hollow
Press

It was the first day of school and Michael was a little nervous.

How will I know where to go after I get off the bus? thought Michael.

Do I go left? Do I go right? Do I go left and then go right? Or maybe...

But before Michael could finish his thought, he looked over his shoulder and saw a little brown spider.

"Oh, hello there, little spider," said Michael.

And down he came.

"It's the first day of school and I don't know which way to go when I get off the bus," Michael told the little spider (who made himself quite comfortable in Michael's hand).

"Do I go left? Do I go right? Do I go left and then right?"

"I know, maybe you can come with me," said Michael. "Will you? Will you come on the bus with me today?"

The Little Brown Spider answered Michael in his own, unique way.

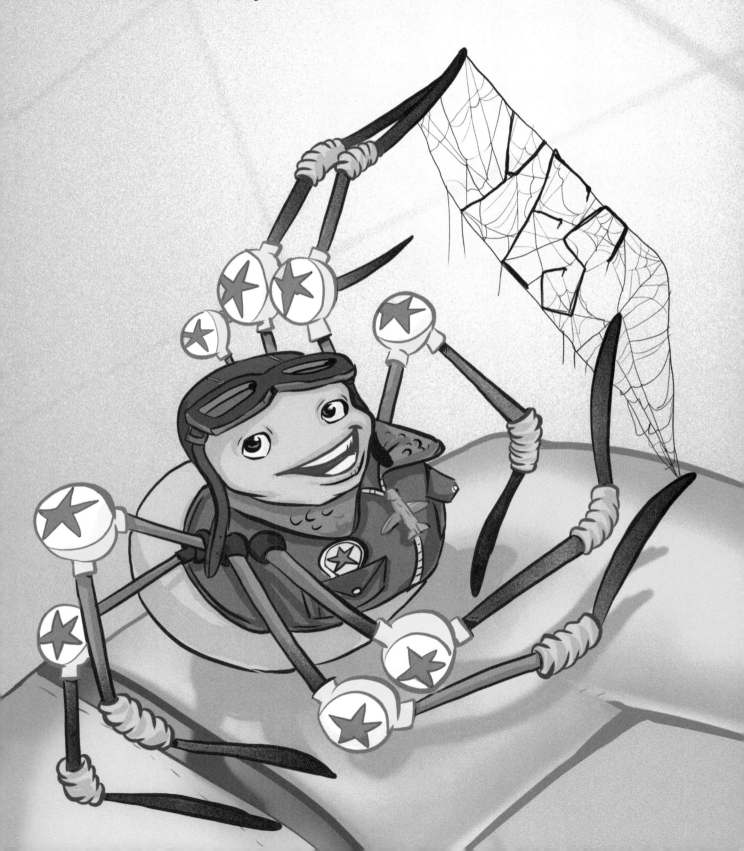

Michael and his new, little friend waited patiently for
the school bus to arrive. And they waited. And waited...

Until, from a distance, they started to hear a rumble.

"The school bus!"

When the big, yellow bus finally stopped at the curb, Michael carefully walked on.

The Little Brown Spider, however, *zipped* on.

As only a spider could!

After Michael sat down, he started to feel a little more nervous. He began to rock back and forth.

Back and forth...

and forth and back...

and back and forth...

and forth and back...

and back and forth...

and forth and back!

All that rocking made the Little Brown Spider quite dizzy!

"How will I know where to go after I get off the bus?" asked Michael. "Which way do I go?"

Michael continued to worry as the bus made its way to school. He imagined all the honking cars and big trucks and speeding motorcycles.

And buses!

It was going to be one, big mess!

And he still didn't know which way to go.

"Do I got left? Do I go right? Or maybe I go left and then right?"

Soon, the bus arrived at school and parked alongside all the other big, yellow buses.

It was time to get off.

Michael got up from his seat and walked nervously to the front of the bus.

He was gently led along by the Little Brown Spider.

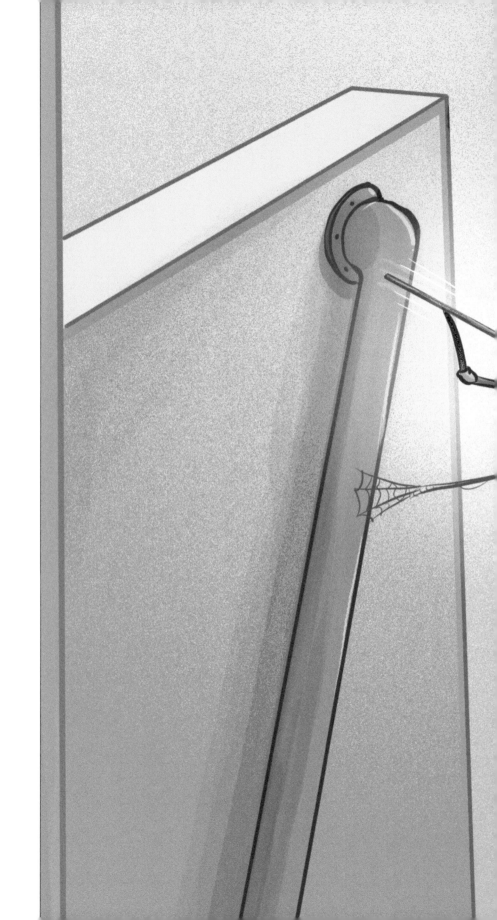

As Michael made his way down the steps of the bus, he started to feel more and more nervous.

How would he know which way to go?

Do I go left when I get off? Do I go right? thought Michael.

Or maybe I go *straight*?

When Michael finally stepped off the bus, he was greeted by a teacher.

In fact, there were a lot of teachers there that day.

And they were all helping the children find their way.

Michael realized he didn't need
to know which way to go after
getting off the school bus.

It wasn't something he needed
to be nervous about at all!

Knowing Michael would be fine getting off the bus from now on, the Little Brown Spider gave his new friend a little tap on the shoulder...

And then set off on his next adventure!